© Nathanaël AMAH , 2020 (**J9CR2L8**)

Cover : Larisa KAZAKOVA

My last night in Siberia

From the same author :

(E-books & paper version)

- Somewhere in Vladivostok
- Harcèlement   *(éd. BOD)*
- Harassment   *(éd. BOD)*
- Acoso   *(éd. BOD)*
- Neith (La mystérieuse Nubienne)   *(éd. BOD)*
- The Nubian (The mysterious Neith)   *(éd. BOD)*
- Les macarons   *(éd. BOD)*
- La veuve PLYNN   *(éd. BOD)*
- Instants ultimes   *(éd. BOD)*
- Que dire de plus ?   *(éd. BOD)*
- Cousine !   *(éd. BOD)*
- *T*u n'es pas la femme de l'homme que je suis   *(éd BOD)*
- Londres : le jour d'après   *(éd BOD)*
- The day after in London   *(éd BOD)*
- Ma dernière nuit en Sibérie   *(éd.BOD)*

(www.bod.fr)

" We triumph over slander just by disdaining it."

My last night in Siberia
© *Nathanaël AMAH , 2020   NATHAM Collection*

MY LAST NIGHT IN SIBERIA

Novel

1

Three months have passed since his arrival in Novosibirsk.

In this Russian city in western Siberia, Jacob BILLIGER is part of a professors exchange program between the United-States and Russia, organized by Novosibirsk State Agrarian University.

Doctor of agronomy, Jacob BILLIGER is the head of the department of ancient cereals at the university of Chicago.

His research successively led him to China, India, Africa and the Middle East. His workhorse: how to adapt cereals to the most extreme climates, to areas with the harshest winters, to the most arid lands. His work has been the subject of numerous publications in reference specialized journals.

Several multinationals rolled out the red carpet to him, without success.

Teaching is his great passion.

A little idealistic, he hopes to get people to take the problem of people's nutrition by the right end : adapt the methods of cultivation, and not to change the nature of cereals. Hence for him, the importance of the rehabilitation of some ancient cereals.

Sometimes he considers himself as a person rowing against the tide, facing agricultural policy of most countries, agricultural policy largely influenced by the more than aggressive activities of lobbyists at the orders of multinationals, in the austere corridors of parliaments.

He realizes that adapting cereals growing method to the specificities of lands or climates does not seem to interest anyone. On the other hand, the temptation for a more immediate, lucrative return is greater, to the detriment of the health of consumers of these products from this type of agriculture of which long-term consequences cannot be measured by no one.

His tenacious character, coupled with an affable nature, allows him to remain faithful to his convictions, even if sometimes, weariness awaits him. On the verge of this predictable weariness, his enthusiasm and persuasiveness take over, boost him and help him capture the attention of his audience, who ends up listening to him almost religiously.

His major concern is to demonstrate the merits of his theory based on scientifically, socially well-supported models. Sometimes he is listened to politely but does not succeed in convincing, sometimes, depending on the country, he gets a benevolent attention, accompanied by a hope of an application, life-size.

Thanks to his notoriety, based on his international reputation, he is well known worldwide. The Russian university had to get in the waiting line before it was able to bring him to Russia for two years. It tried to get him to come in Russia , in order to find out a little more about this atypical agronomist engineer, full of common sense, and to try to understand why he is both adored and decried.

To make up its own mind, and possibly to question itself: the university's leadership does not lack courage in the face of the ruling party's line in agricultural politics, namely, not to lose sight of Russia's ambition to once again become the grain granary of the planet as in this glorious past of the Soviet era.

Thus, giving Russia the ability to re-influence the price of grain on world markets would be consistent with the party politics.

2

Upon his arrival in Novosibirsk, he was surprised by the welcome he received.

During the introductory meeting, the director of the research program was quick to make the deal clear. In exchange for the broad facilities that would be granted to him to understand Russia's agricultural politics from the inside, he would have to give him a synthesis of the models that have been the subject of his publications, in particular, the sharing of ownership of agricultural lands.

My last night in Siberia

The Director is well aware that the purpose of his application is only a small part of his guest's research topics. But he needs an informed opinion to consolidate an eminently political issue to be handed over to the Minister of Agriculture, very soon.

Things are clear : under the guise of welcoming a specialist as part of a project of exchange professors between two major countries, Jacob BILLIGER finds himself in the role of a political consultant. A mission in the mission.

He is involuntarily the missing link in a state apparatus of whose he does not know the ins and outs. The perfect cover while, it begins to be said in multinationals that, Jacob BILLIGER is in Russia.

One day, in front of his building, as he was about to go to the grocery store to fill the mini refrigerator of his studio in which he is housed, he was apostrophized by a young man who at first glance seemed to know him, by speaking directly to him in English.

Since his arrival, no one had spoken directly to him in English, apart from the PhD students with whom he should collaborate and who are perfectly bilingual.

- " *Good evening Mr. BILLIGER.*"

- " *Good evening. Who are you? What do you want from me?* "

- " *My name wouldn't tell you anything. I'm being sent by friends who want to talk to you about your mission.* "

- " *Friends? ... What do you mean ?* "

- " *Would you be willing to meet them?* "

- " *You're wrong about me. I'm in a hurry. Goodbye sir.* "

- " *No Mr. BILLIGER. I'm not mistaken about you. Would you be willing to meet my friends? If I was you, I wouldn't hesitate.* "

- " *You are not in my shoes. Goodbye sir.* "

- " ***You're the one who sees it. I'm so sorry I bothered you. Goodbye Mr. BILLIGER. See you soon. my name is Igor. See you soon.*** "

That said, the mysterious Igor walked away.

He remains for a short moment frozen, surprised at the content of this surreal discussion that he has just had, and then, watching him walk away, he tries to remember if, he has already met this individual at university. To no avail. Then he goes back to the grocery store before it closes.

3

Back in his apartment, Jacob puts away the groceries. A moment of relaxation before starting the preparation of dinner. He turns on the TV. Supreme privilege attached to his position: he can get CNN. Keeping in touch with the Usa is essential for him. Waiting for the news, a little glass of vodka. A second one. He's not far from drunkenness. He needs to eat something. He decides to prepare the dinner, his TV still is working.

Two beautiful slices of salmon trout,

accompanied by a few blinis warmed in a double boiler.

He sits quietly in front of the TV, the bottle of vodka at hand, the meal tray well stuck in his lap.

Dinner can finally begin.

Suddenly, before he had time to fill his third glass of vodka, the apartment phone began to ring. This is the first time this phone has ringed at night since he arrived. He takes a look at his watch. 9:10 p.m. Who can it be?

He places the tray on the coffee table, then picks up the handset.

He stays silent. He waits for a few seconds and then, at the other end of the line :

- " *Hello!* "

On first listen, the voice of his interlocutor does not tell him anything. A man's voice, all the most banal.

- "***Hello !**"* he said with some restraint.

- " ***Good evening Mr BILLIGER**.* "

He can't believe it. He thinks he recognizes the voice. He can't believe it.

- " ***Good evening. Who do I have the honour to talk to?*** " he responds by trying to regain control of the situation.

Against all odds, he hears a laugh at the other end of the line. Then **:**

- " ***Mr BILLIGER, it's Igor. Do you remember me? We spoke a few moments ago.*** "

- " ***Yes. What do you want from me?*** " he said dryly.

- " ***Nothing. It's just to wish you a good night. Good night Mr. BILLIGER. See you soon.*** "

The interlocutor, called Igor, has just hung up.

What about this sudden incursion of this person into his life? And twice in a row in the same day. What does it mean?

He's still stunned. It is not in his habits to allow himself to be invaded by such emotions. He has seen more in his life as a speaker. He is not a man to be intimidated. And it is not this little Mr. Igor who will be able to prevent him from tasting his salmon trout and having a good evening.

4

After a halftone night, he awoke a little disturbed by the events of the day before that have unlocked something in him.

Indeed, during his wanderings around the world, he has sometimes been approached by individuals, charged with making him understand things half-word, sometimes in more subtle ways, other times by using open-faced harassment.

He recalls his curious meeting with this Nigerian businessman who came to attend one of his conferences in Lagos, very cultured, very friendly, visibly well introduced to the upper political spheres of the country, frequenting the head of state, equipped with the best intentions of the world, presumably interested in the potential that could offer the rehabilitation of old cereals for the development of his sub-region , but who in the end turned out to be the masked emissary of a multinational on Nigerian territory.

It was a great disappointment for him.

Not for being abused by this man (to whom he had given all his trust, who had almost become a friend to whom he could go as at house), but for the irreparable loss of this great opportunity that could have allowed Nigeria to be an open-air laboratory, the spearhead in the service of a suitable agriculture within sub-Saharan Africa as a whole and thus contribute to the resolution of the many problems of induced nutrition caused by famines.

He cannot bring himself to consider that, man (human being) can be a permanent danger to himself.

Through sessions of questions/answers post lectures, he was able to observe (by finely analyzing the exchanges with participants or the governing bodies during the hearings granted in the ministries), the propensity that man has to never consider things as a whole.

In technical files, he reads "individual" instead of "community," he reads "profit" instead of "benefit," he reads "consume" instead of "renew."

Such is the life of man.

Fighting against this, is a titanic work.
He's well aware of that.
He has been working courageously on it for years, in the manner of a utopian who set out to grass the surface of the earth square centimeter by square centimeter.

He has not been overly concerned about this sudden change in his daily life since his arrival in Novosibirsk.

However, he cannot help but wonder at the moment what lies out behind the incursion of this individual who tries to intrude into his life, like a pebble in his shoe.

5

Back to university.

As the bus arrived into Akademgorodok (the academic city, the aptly named Silicon Taiga), travelling the hundred meters that separate the bus stop from the main entrance of the old university building, Jacob comes face to face with his worst nightmare, Mr. Igor who has just left the university compound.

So he's in university, he thinks . But in what

capacity? Student? Employee?

Igor, it's like John in England or Bernard in France. A common name, carried by the greatest number. How can he know who this person is? You might as well look for a needle in a straw boot.

- " *Hello Mr BILLIGER. Have a nice day.* "

he said with a broad smile as he crossed paths with him.

He seems to savor the unease that is gradually taking hold in this dear Mr. BILLIGER. Worse, he's having fun. While continuing to play his role perfectly in this machination that is going on, like the spider that patiently weaves its web around the unwisely misplaced insect,he does not lose sight of the object of his mission.

What is his exact role in this university, knowing that he is neither a Doctoral student nor a staff member? But then, what was he doing inside the university just as Jacob was getting off the bus?

- " *Hello. Do you have a minute?* "

Jacob told him when he met him.

- " *Yes with pleasure Mr BILLIGER. What can I do for you ?* "

Always so kind this dear Igor.

- " *Who are you? What do you want from me? I would like to have some answers today.* "

Igor sketches a broad and beautiful smile, as usual.

- " *I'm Igor as you know ...* "

Jacob interrupts him.

- " *Igor what? What's your last name?* "

adds Jacob visibly angry.

- " *Nothing could be simpler Mr. BILLIGER. If you want to know who I am, accept our invitation. Agree to meet my friends.* "

he said, with a smile on his face. What deeply annoys Jacob who is about to come out of his hinges.

- " *What the hell are you talking about? What invitation?* "

- " *My friends want to meet you. They insist a lot. Please Mr BILLIGER, do not disappoint them. I'm begging you.* "

- " *Stop your gibberish and leave me alone !* "

- " *Otherwise? Think carefully, Mr. BILLIGER, before it's too late.* "

Exasperated, Jacob does not respond to what he considers to be a final provocation of this uninteresting individual, shrugging and entering the university area without looking back.

6

Sitting at his desk, Jacob struggles to start his day. His anger doesn't go away. He does not like to be deprived of his freedom, which is basically enshrined in his DNA, as a free man and as an American citizen, moreover on Russian soil.

He likes his mission He feels lucky to be in this place that allows him to enrich his doctrine. A nice reference for his lecturer and teacher status. Working in Russia on such a project deserves special attention. He cannot therefore tolerate the slightest intrusion into what he considers to be his square meadow.

It is not in his character to give in to blackmail, neither emotional nor of any kind. According to him, the breeding ground for blackmail is the ability of everyone to listen carefully to the blackmailer. The best antidote: to reveal "his/her" truth to the face of the world.

What he should already have done.

He picks up his phone and asks for an interview with the project director. It must find an ideal angle of attack to objectively expose the situation as it presents itself, without being noticed, without creating unease within the university, since he cannot even identify the famous Igor and provide an accurate description of him.

Moreover, on what basis will he support his allegations?

An individual invites you to meet his friends.

So what? Is it so complicated to say yes or no? Is there anything to whip a cat?

What is at stake is very important for the future of his mission : his credibility. Yes, but what will be the cost ?

Some might object that: "*The veracity of an assertion has nothing to do with his credibility...* »

Okay, but isn't it his paranoia that could jeopardize his credibility and not the pitiful gesticulations of the mysterious Igor?

Besides, where does paranoia begin, where does caution end? In other words, what is the line between prudence and paranoia?

In any case, he is world-famous. He's respected. He's being listened to. He cannot afford to draw attention to himself in this way and create risk provoking a diplomatic incident between Russia and the United States.

And then heck ! Let him go to hell.

He picks up the handset and cancels his interview request, and gets to work.

The day takes place without problem in a newfound inner peace. He is fine-tuning a report on the management of agricultural land.

7

The day ends. He puts his things in his satchel. But just before leaving the office, the project director bursts into his office.

- " *All is ok ? How's it going?* "

- " *Yes all is ok, Mr. Director.* "

- " *Did you want to see me, what it seems?* "

- " *Yes, Mr. Director, but on reflection, I have given it up.* "

33   *My last night in Siberia*
© *Nathanaël AMAH , 2020   NATHAM Collection*

- " Do you have a problem? "

- " No, Mr. Director. ... I wanted to hear your opinion on something. Three times nothing. "

- " Okay Mr. BILLIGER. Ok. I want you to know that my door is open to you. Good evening. "

- "Thank you. Good evening, Mr. Director. "

The director leaves the office and closes the door behind him. Jacob sits down. He reflects on this missed opportunity. Informal communication could have been appropriate in such a situation. Just have his opinion on the attitude to adopt. But he is in Russia and not in the United States of America where, it is possible to knock on the director's door, submit a concern to him and ask for his help to solve it. However, he does not know, if in Russia, the informal can at any time turn to the formal by the simple act of expressing things. And what are the consequences ultimately for him, for his mission in solid gold, or even for his credibility?

He does not know.

In the face of the director, caution was the most appropriate option. He had no choice.

He finishes tidying up his stuff and then gets out of his office. In the hallway, he meets a doctoral student to whom he had been introduced upon his arrival. He stops for a few minutes to greet her and hear from her. Brief discussion and promise to meet again very soon in the framework of the project.

At the bus station. The bus is announced in twenty minutes.

Some students are waiting like him. And suddenly, while he was lost in his thoughts, he sees out of the university compound, Igor in great conversation with the doctoral student with whom he had just discussed.

He doest not have a bad vision. It's Igor and she's the doctoral student.

So, all Jacob BILLIGER he is, the most listened to man in his field of competence, and who has his head well screwed on his shoulders, he cannot help but fall back into what should be called ordinary and inevitable paranoia. The one which threatens and insinuates itself into the spirit of the one who does not feel neither anguish nor fear, but who lives in ignorance of what is happening in reality. For him, seeing Igor and the doctoral student together is necessarily a sign that something is going on his back. Enough to fuel his fantasies and his future insomnia.

36

My last night in Siberia
© *Nathanaël AMAH , 2020 NATHAM Collection*

8

He goes home, a little disturbed, extremely concerned about the idea that something is going on, something of which he doesn't know anything about.

To make matters worse, on the way home, the concierge informed him (as she could, in bad English), that, moments before his return, two people had come to visit him.

Two people!? Why, he wonders. He doesn't know anyone. He doesn't hang out with anyone.

The janitor was not able (as he would have liked) to specify whether it was a man and a woman. This information would have allowed him to have some certainties, in response to his questioning about Igor and the doctoral student. But on second thought, it cannot be. They didn't get on the bus. So they couldn't (logically) get to the studio before him. Therefore, back to square one. The need for urgent discussions with the Director is a distressing return to the agenda.

Very bad evening ahead. He doesn't like it. He doesn't even want to turn on the TV. CNN will wait. News from the country will also wait. He doesn't want anything. He is not hungry. He just wants a drink or two.

He thought he was strong and invincible behind his desk as a distinguished speaker, with his remarkable intelligence in front of his audience.

A perfectly identified and predictable audience that he must face with arguments.

But the torment in which he has gradually locked himself in, and which makes him tremble like a leaf in front of this invisible enemy, makes him extremely nervous.

None of his skills, none of his knowledge can put out this fire that begins to consume him from the inside, little by little.

A question arises: why is he resolutely trying to link Igor to a hypothetical cabal mounted against his person?

Only he knows.

Is paranoia invading his mind?

Yet, he is not a man who can be   impressed.

Is it because he's in Russia? Is it this phantasmagorial around Russia that, over time, has built this reputation as a country in which every citizen is a potential spy?

If so, why did he accept the university's kind invitation to be included in this professor exchange programme between the two countries? No one had forced him to integrate this process or forced him to accept this mission.

It was a well-considered decision, warmly encouraged by the University of Chicago and welcomed by Novossibirsk State Agrarian University.

Is he regretting this decision?

Yet, the first three months of the mission took place in ideal conditions of physical and mental comfort. He was even willing to accept an extension of the duration of his stay in Russia, so much, the mission is beautiful, vast, intellectually rewarding. Who can claim to have at his disposal an open-air laboratory, laboratory in which all the technical and social data allow optimal exploitation in a climate of sincerity and cordiality? He has this chance to claim that. He is proud and honored.

His joy is like this pride-tinged joy felt by children in front of a beautiful toy on Christmas Day, lived on until that famous day when, Igor entered his life.

9

Upon his arrival at the office the next morning, he found a message from the director's secretary informing him that he was being summoned to the director's office in the early afternoon.

He reads and rereads the message several times.

Since the beginning of his mission, it has never happened for him, to be called or summoned by the director, through this channel. This is not usual.

A scheduled meeting with the director is announced in the department's electronic calendar, accessible to the entire team, and not on a piece of paper deposited on the desks.

He logs on to the electronic calendar, but finds no mention of that "interview" with the director scheduled for early afternoon.

As a summons, he cannot accept or refuse to go there. He has no choice. He has to go there.

He thought for a moment of this specific, informal request from the Director regarding the creation of the famous file to be handed over to the Minister.

This is not plausible. His request is almost confidential, and he would not venture to use the secretary channel to process an order from the Minister.

All the hypotheses are reviewed one after the other, to no avail.

What's the point of tormenting himself. In a few hours, he will know more. For now, the hardest part is getting to focus on his morning agenda.

2 p.m.

In front of the director's office. Jacob knocks at the door.

- " *Voydite ! "*   (Come in !)

Hearing these words and without understanding their meaning, Jacob thought it was appropriate to open the door and enter the office. He closed the door behind him.

- " *Oh, is that you ?* " (said the director, looking up).

- "   *Yes, Mr Director. I received your summons this morning.* "

- "   *Yes Mr BILLIGER. Well, I wanted to speak with you about a sensitive and extremely troubling matter.* "

- " *I'm listening to you, Mr Director.* "

- " *Mr. BILLIGER, can you tell me why are the police investigating you?* "

coldly questions the director, staring him in the eye.

Jacob blushed.

- " *An investigation about me? It's impossible, Mr Director. This must be a misunderstanding.* "

he said in a trembling voice.

- " *Yet, it seems so, Mr BILLIGER. ... They went to your house last night. Have you not been informed about this visit?* "

- " *I learned that two people came to visit me just before I returned, nothing more. The concierge was not able to tell me more. I don't speak Russian and she doesn't speak English.* "

- " *Tell me Mr BILLIGER, who have you*

My last night in Siberia

been dating with since you arrived in Novosibirsk? It looks like you've made relationships with some people. A hell of relationship, it seems. You haven't wasted your time. I do not know what to think about this situation and your future at our university. "

Jacob feels like he's living a nightmare. His mouth became dry. Ideas jostle in his head. The desire to leave and go home to Chicago on the spot crossed his mind for a moment. But he needs to get back on his feet and try (if there is still time to do so) to clean his honor of any suspicion. The stakes are huge.

10

The heated and surreal discussion between the director and Jacob ended abruptly. Indeed, the presence of the director was required in an important meeting at the other part of the central building.

Upon his return to his office, Jacob applied for two days off to the director for personal reasons.

The director agreed and granted him the

whole week.

He can't help but give him this week off, and admits that Jacob needs time and calm to manage the situation. He imagines himself alone in the Usa, mired in a case beyond his comprehension, without any recourse, without any help.

However, he does not understand how a man of his reputation could have compromised himself to this extent.

He cannot accept that, Mr BILLIGER, the world-renowned international expert, can be an impostor who works for a foreign power as it's whispered.

These allegations seem implausible or even fanciful to him, since it is Russia which certainly needs to exploit his knowledge and not the other way around.

This professorship program between Russia and the United States is similar to a partnership agreement in which everyone brings and receives. A partnership described as a good conduct pact in which the rule of fairness applies in all its rigour. A win-win agreement in which each partner has an obligation to also be concerned about the interests of the other partner, which is fairly in favour of its own interests.

This totally excludes tricking for the purpose of providing false information to the detriment of the other partner, for an unspoken purpose of sabotaging the data and its exploitation.

In any case, he waits for a clear explanation before referring it to his hierarchy, if necessary. If this is really necessary. To this end, he prepares a preliminary report on the case and puts it under the elbow.

 The director had weighed in all his weight for the admission of Professor Emeritus Jacob BILLIGER in the professors exchange program. Therefore, he has no desire to have to justify his choice before his hierarchy. He can't admit that he was wrong about him. And he knows he wasn't wrong. But he needs to prove it. He doesn't want to have to answer phone calls at the milkman's time.

Back in his apartment, Jacob tries to regain his serenity, convinced that there is an explanation for what is happening to him.

But above all, he must find Igor who has vanished into nature, as if by enchantment, now that the damage is done.

How's he going to do it ?

He doesn't speak Russian and he doesn't know anyone in Novosibirsk.

Dear reader,

At this point in story, what would you have done if you were in Jacob BILLIGER's situation ? Would you be able to write the rest of this story?

Yes ?

So, please sit down, take a sheet of paper, a pen and enjoy yourself.

Then pick up again my book, go to the next pages and read the rest of this incredible story.

Compare!

11

Returning a little earlier, Jacob takes advantage of this afternoon, "in semi-freedom, the bridle on his neck" to stroll around his neighborhood while caressing the secret hope of meeting Igor on his way.

You might as well look for a needle in a haystack.

He wanders through the city like a soul in pain, his satchel in   hand.

Not Igor's shadow on the horizon.

Here he is in the street SOVIETSKAÏA, a stone's throw from St. Alexander-NEVSKI Cathedral.

Machinally, he enters the cathedral to pray.

It doesn't look like him, he, the cartesian spirit who refuses metaphysics, he who does not have faith, to pray in such a place.

Yet, he needs this moment of silence and this moment of recollection.

He has a burning question.

Do the angels have the answer?

Nothing is less certain.

He always thought that God would be a pure illusion in the service of those who flee devil and its mysteries.

So, prostrate on this bench in the last row at the back of the cathedral, what differentiates him from those men and women whom he has always avoided rubbing shoulders with so as not to compromise himself with their exalted fervors?

In other words, what could be this common denominator that brings them together in this place at this very moment if it's not the fear of the unknown?

A form of collegiality in the face of the "devil" (generic sense): for some, identify and solve existential difficulties, for others, try to understand the suddenness of an event or situation that overwhelms them.

He remembers the words of one of his students in the United States with whom he often discussed about "God" and who said to him in essence, paraphrasing and adapting a Thought of Shakespeare, namely **:**

" *... If you don't have God in you, you're a traitor. And traitors are always punished one day .* "

Has the time for his punishment come? Is Igor

his punishment?

Yet, he does not consider himself as a traitor. He does not meddle in God's affairs, either near or far. Nor he does not consider himself as an opportunist by finding himself in this place in which God is the last resort when the understanding of the human being has reached its apogee.

Here he is in a paradoxical dialogue with himself: he, the engineer with the Cartesian spirit, he, the great BILLIGER, creator of a world-famous doctrine, imbued with himself, mastering his science to perfection, but today, stopped in his greatness by a persistent rumor, a banal rumor that obliges him to keep a low profile and adopt a position tinged with great humility.

Some would say that, it is not the time of his punishment which has arrived, but that of his awakening, the awakening of his necessary humility.

12

The return of the prodigal child to the father's house, welcomed with kindness despite his terrible arrogance in the face of life. His presence in this place is an unlikely event in the life of the one who advocates self-sufficiency at all levels, both spiritual and temporal.

Still prostrate on his bench at the back of the cathedral, he is   immersed in a kind of reverie for a few minutes when, sounds of footsteps slamming heavily on the ground, bring him back to reality.

He straightens his head, and looks a little closer. He saw a group of four soldiers, heading a clocked step towards the central nave of the cathedral.

He watches them move away and suddenly an idea crossed his mind.

Why didn't he think of it before?

If the police are investigating him, then why not go in person, directly to the source of the information at the police premises?

It's worth what it's worth.

But he feels relieved to have found this beginning of the track to decant the situation.

A spontaneous solicitation towards the police is better than a warrant to bring issued against him.

He thus avoids the inconvenience of harsh

treatment methods applied by sworn agents entangled in the religion of the law.

He cannot afford the supreme luxury of a high-profile arrest that could irreparably damage his reputation and jeopardize the continuation of his prestigious mission at the university.

He takes a look at his watch. It's about 5:00 pm. He thinks for a moment. It's too late to go to the police station. On the other hand, not speaking Russian, he needs to prepare two or three sentences allowing him to announce the purpose of his visit to the police premises. For the interpretation, he will see on the spot with the persons responsible for investigating his case, unless they are perfectly bilingual.

He gets up quickly, heads for the exit and cannot help but say with humility : "THANK YOU" as he walks through the big door of the cathedral.

"Thank you" to whom and for what reason ? He doesn't know, but he felt a urge to say it, at the moment he left the cathedral.

He feels like a patient of whom suddenly the health gets better as soon as the doctor's appointment is set. Well-known psychological effect demonstrating the power of the mind over the body. He, so tired at the moment of his entrance into the cathedral, feel now less demoralized, inflated to block, ready to fight, already convinced that, he'll be totally cleared of all the suspicions that weigh on him.

13

On the way back, he can't wait to get back to the apartment to write the two or three introductory sentences at the police office.

When he arrived at the apartment, he immediately got down to work. Dinner can wait.

For more coherence and clarity insofar as he will not be able to speak Russian, he performs in the first place and in English, the detailed account of the events that occurred since his first meeting with Igor until his interview with the project director on the university premises.

He puts his text clean in case, the russian investigators would like (through his document) to have a first idea on the unfolding of the facts before deciding whether or not, they must continue their investigation on him.

But as he reread the document, he thinks of a multitude of such important questions in relation to each other.

The document he has just drafted would be entirely in accordance with custom in the United States regarding the relationship between citizens and their police.

But what will happen in Russia about this document in the hands of the Russian police?

How can we know whether what is recorded in his document would not be harmful to him in this country about which he knows nothing about how to behave with the authorities of the judicial police?

Should he strictly remain factual and avoid expressing feelings?

Should he avoid drafting a document that could be exploited against him?

Is it absolutely necessary to be wary of the apriorism of the investigators charged with providing the evidence which will certainly, support and confirm the conclusions already pre-established?

Yet, he should not be asking all these questions.
He has to stay confident.
By definition and above all, Russia is a country of law like most so-called developed countries.

What could he be afraid of ?

He is not an ordinary person on Russian soil : he is the guest of the country and as such, he should not be at all moved by the poor gesticulations of a scoundrel probably in the pay of some private interests in the country or internationally.

Certainty?

Supputation ?

Or simply, an effective way to give himself courage before his confrontation with the police, he, the famous, the respected Jacob BILLIGER?

Sitting at his table in front of his document a thousand and one times reread, lost in his thoughts, it's the time for him, (and for the first time in his life), to question himself, to see himself as he is, without artifice, nor adorned with his glory conferred by his clothes of scholar, weakened by a tiny "insect" that came to buzz around his ears and thus disturb his tranquillity in his pleasantly tidy life. Here he is again a " Man ", an ordinary man, a litigant not above suspicion.

14

It's getting late.

He made the decision to prepare his dinner.

Here he is in front of the stove, trying to concentrate on his preparation. No frills, just the minimum   for an acceptable and balanced meal that he devours like a hungry robot.

After this quickly engulfed dinner, he pushed

his plate and cutlery aside, then took his document for a final rereading before getting ready for the night.

During this final rereading, another idea germinated in his mind.

As an American citizen on Russian soil, the best he can do, would it not be to contact his embassy in Moscow to be assisted?

Rich idea that would put an end to his torment. Yes, but such an approach would involve two states and could provoke the shutdown of this teacher exchange program. Above all, Jacob cares about his mission for the reasons you already know.

The next day, after a surprisingly quiet night and a frugal breakfast quickly taken, he is ready to go to the police premises.

He checks one last time that his document is tidy in his satchel.

At this very moment when he is about to return to the street, his confidence capital is at its best level. He has absolutely no regrets about accepting this mission, for which he is ready to face all the police in the world to defend his honour. He feels no remorse for choosing to write his document rather than use the diplomatic route to solve his problem. And curiously, he has blind confidence in the outcome of his interview with investigators.

Here's in a few words, what his state of mind sums up on this cold morning.

He beckons a taxi and he is driven to the police station. He pays and heads to the entrance.

A first difficulty : he must pass the roadblock of the two policemen in front of the police station. From his pocket, he pulls a piece of paper and hands it to one of the policemen on duty.

- " *Доброе утро, сэр, я американский горожанин. Я не говорю по-русски. Я хотела бы встретиться с офицером. Могу я войти?* "

My last night in Siberia

(Good morning, sir. I'm an American citizen. I don't speak Russian. I'd like to speak to an officer. Can I come in?)

After going through the contents of the paper, the officer stares at him for a short time and then approaches his colleague and hands him the paper.
After reading it, the second policeman asked him with some authority and in English :

- " ***Passport, please ! ***"

He obeys and hands him his passport.

After a cursory check, the officer invites him to follow him inside the police station, instructs him to wait for him in the waiting room and disappears into a maze of corridors.

15

After a very long wait, the policeman reappears and asks him to wait and then goes out to join his colleague.

Nearly two hours later, a uniformed policewoman shows up and asks him to follow her.

It's about time. He was beginning to find the time long, almost regretting getting into this situation. Nor he could get up and go. His passport is being held somewhere in one of the offices. He can easily imagine the excitement he unleashed when he showed up at the police station.

With a hesitant step, he follows the policewoman who walks fast through the maze of corridors.

A moment later, the policewoman makes a stop and knocks on a door. She waits for the green light.

She was ordered to get in. She opens the door and enters into the office. She salutes. She invites Jacob to get in, in his turn.

He complies and enters the office. The policewoman goes out of the office and closes the door behind her.

Jacob finds himself alone, facing three people sitting on the same side of the desk. Two of them in uniform, the third in light grey suits.

The person in the suit invites him (in a perfect English) to sit in the chair opposite.

He thanks him with a nod, takes his seat and waits for the rest.

He understood that this person in a grey suit was the interpreter and that, they had to wait for his arrival before receiving him. This could explain the two hours of waiting, unless ..... . He waits to see.

- *"You wanted to talk to an officer. The senior officer and his deputy here, have agreed to listen to you. I'm going to do the translation. My name is Dimitri."*

Jacob leans to the side, grabs his satchel , puts it on his lap. He opens it and pulls out his precious document.

- *" I would like to thank the officer and his deputy for agreeing to receive me without an appointment.*
My name is Jacob BILLIGER, I am part of the professor exchange program between Russia and the United States.
To the extent that I do not speak Russian, I have taken the liberty of writing a brief to outline the purpose of my visit to your

administration. "

That said, he stands up and hands the document to the senior officer.

All talk together and then, the deputy picks up the handset and talks to someone.

A minute later, the uniformed policewoman knocks on the door and stands in the doorway.

- " *The secretary will take you back to the waiting room. We need a little time to read and understand your document.* "

adds the interpreter.

Jacob gets up, walks past the secretary who closes the office door. She takes him back to the waiting room and invites him to sit down.

16

An hour later, the interpreter appears before him.

Jacob gets up and makes himself available.

- " *We have looked at your paper. Go home. We'll get in touch with you in a few days. Here's your passport. Have a good day Mr BILLIGER.* "

- " *Thank you. Goodbye Mr DIMITRI.* "

On these civilities, the two men leave each other. Dimitri disappears into the maze of corridors, Jacob heads for the exit.

What he feels at this very moment is the satisfaction of having anticipated the reaction of the police regarding the investigation on him.

According to him, the mere fact of introducing himself spontaneously to the police, half-innocents him. This proves (always according to him) that he has nothing to hide.

But nothing is less certain.

On the other hand, how to understand the terse message of the interpreter who instructs him to go home and to wait for the police summons him? A kind of house arrest? No, he gave him his passport back. The sign that they trust him? Yes, he believes it, sincerely.

In Jacob's brain, ideas mingle confusedly, taking turns moving from a state of extreme optimism to that of the depressive who has touched the bottom without the slightest hope of being able to go back up the slope, deprived of the necessary motor energy.

The idea of a possible resignation crossed his mind, but his pride and legendary arrogance quickly ruled out this possibility.

Jacob BILLIGER does not resign.

He does not want and cannot perish under the blows of an invisible enemy.

In that case, his proved mortal enemy is not Igor and his "friends". It is this weariness which is watching him and which potentially could push him to this resignation that is not (from his point of view) on the agenda.

Yet, he finds himself in this relationship of permanent interlocution with himself on the need to let go of his arrogance in order to see and apprehend reality in this country like no other.

He remains adamant.

He cannot let go of this arrogance which is deeply inscribed in his DNA because of the generosity that characterizes him in the sharing of his knowledge with others, his prodigalities (his excessive implications in the agricultural polics of the States which do him the honor of listening to him), which naturally lead him to this arrogant attitude.

His friends are thousands of miles away. Towards Who to turn if not himself in the face of adversity? Some would say that, if there is no adversity, success would not have that pleasant flavor that we can experience.

In any case, caution is required.

Loneliness weighs on him. How to get away from it?

He walks here and there for hours through Novossibirsk, like a robot, his satchel in hand, the sad face, the step badly insured.

17

He ends up taking a taxi to drop him off at his home.

It's about 3 p.m. It has nothing in the stomach. He needs to eat something quickly. He's having a hypoglycemia attack. He opens the refrigerator. There is not much. He still manages to prepare a meal tray. He'll have to go out for some food shopping before dark.

9 p.m.

It's dark outside. The weather is very cool, almost cold. It's late fall. A time when, (with winter announcing its advent), everyone stays warm at home.

In his sofa, Jacob takes advantage of this free time to delve into reading some recently arrived magazines from the United States. Subjects that do not really interest him, but he tries to read to allow him to occupy his mind and succumb to this nervous fatigue that he drags for a few days.

1 a.m.

Exhausted, he falls asleep.

5 a.m.

Still in his deep sleep, Jacob suddenly is awakened by repeated blows to his door.

He opens his eyes and tries to understand what's going on. He turns on his bedside lamp and looks at the alarm clock.

He first thought of a fire in the building. He

gets up and rushes to the door, while the blows continue to be struck on the door. He finally opens the door.

What was his surprise to see in front of him, a group of people, some in civilian clothes, others, in uniform, weapon in hand.

His heart began to beat very fast.

As soon as he opens the door, the uniformed people rush into the appartment, and put him against the wall under good guard.

His first reaction, repeating in a loop **:**

- "   *I want to talk to my embassy!*   "

No one's answering him.

Seconds later, the interpreter from the previous day at the police station, in turn enters the appartment. He approaches him, stares at him for a moment, then tells him **:**

- " *Homeland Security has signed a search warrant. We are here to carry out that mandate. "*

Jacob's taken aback.

- " ***Homeland security? .... What did I do?
What does that mean? "***

- " ***I'm not allowed to tell you. You will
know more in the premises of the territorial
security. "***

- " ***Call my embassy! "***

shouts Jacob.

- " ***There's no point in yelling. The embassy
will be informed on time. For now, Allow us
to do our job and, for the last time,   stop
shouting. "***

responds the interpreter dryly.

Then, the officers in uniform, conduct a
methodical and thorough search, going so far
as to inspect the inside of his shoes, creating
and leaving a real chaos behind them.

They confiscate his laptop and various documents related to his mission.

Jacob observes the scene he is witnessing, wondering on which planet he is on.

After a full hour of this violent psychological torture, in agreement with the head of the commando, the interpreter orders him to dress (under good guard) for the purpose of his transfer to the premises of the territorial security, handcuffed to the wrists.

18

Arriving under good escort in the premises of the territorial security, Jacob is at first isolated in a room in which he is detached, his left hand immediately attached again to an iron hook sealed in the wall in a corner of the room.

Occasionally, an armed officer opens the door and checks that everything is in order in the room.

My last night in Siberia
© *Nathanaël AMAH , 2020   NATHAM Collection*

The hands of the clock turn endlessly throughout the morning. Jacob has neither water nor food.

He, Jacob BILLIGER adulated, respected, listened, accustomed to the most upscale palaces, the most expensive, the most luxurious, now sitting on a chair fixed to the ground, attached to an iron hook in the premises of the territorial security like a vulgar criminal.

How did he arrived to this point? Only his audition will allow him to know more. For now, no embassy, no lawyer. He is alone, desperately alone in the face of his future in this matter that is beyond his comprehension.

Around noon, the same agent returned to the room with a sandwich and a small bottle of water, which he placed at his feet on the floor and left without having talked to him.

He went down lower than a dog that receives its food in his bowl. He, he has received his food on the ground, like a wretch to whom the remains of the table are thrown.

At this point, to eat or not to eat, what does it matter?

In his situation, he no longer knows which world he belongs to : the one of the living or the one of the dead ? The one of men or that of animals ?

Instinct of survival obliges, he manages to catch the small bottle of water by the neck and quenches his thirst. His mouth being terribly dry, he cannot keep the water in his mouth, which dripps on his sweater. He puts down the bottle and tries hard to wipe the water drops on his sweater. He wips away a tear with the back of his free hand.

Greatness and decadence !

What was his life all about?

Appearing, grabbing the light of fame, touching the heights of glory, dispensing his knowledge. To be the one who knows, the one who is listened to with respect even if you don't agree with him.

Now, for the second time in a short time, he looks up to heaven to beg for the help of divine providence.

What can it do for him at this very moment? Does it have the right to speak in this place? What is its room for manoeuvre in this space isolated inside the territorial security premises ?

Will the thickness of the walls allow his plea to God to pass?

Will his sudden fervor (probably inspired by his guardian angel) effectively erase those years of spiritual self-sufficiency coupled with an undeniable arrogance, to the point of ignoring God's existence?

19

2 p.m.

Two armed officers enter the room. They approach him. One of them pulls a key out of his pocket and unlocks Jacob's handcuff from the iron hook, and ties it to his own wrist.

He tells him something in Russian, then makes him get up. All three of them go out of the room.

In the maze of corridors, they stop in front of a door. The officer with his hands free, opens the door and inspects the premises. He gives the green light to his colleague who brings Jacob into the toilets.

For the first time, he has experienced the most painful and the most surreal experience : he was obliged to take his sex out of his trousers with his free hand, in order to relieve himself in front of people, his other hand, attached to the armed guardian's hand.

Fortunately, nature is well made. All he had to do was to wait a little while concentrating, and he manages to relieve himself by emptying his bladder ready to explode. He puts his sex into his pants, and asks to get closer to the bathroom sink to wash his dirty hand, in default of be able to cleanse his body in its entirety of all the stains accumulated on him since dawn. The armed gardian accepts and allows him to wash his dirty hand.

Then, as before entering the toilets, the other officer goes out first and gives the green light. They emerge from the toilets and redirect to the secluded room.

Verification procedure, then resettlement of the accused Jacob BILLIGER under the same conditions.

9 p.m.

A sandwich and half a bottle of water, served in the same conditions of contempt.

Now, at his feet, two salmon sandwiches lying pitifully in their freshness packaging.

Too proud to pick up his food from the ground, Jacob refuses to give in to the hunger that grips him. However, he has to eat something. He's diabetic. He doesn't know where he is with his blood sugar rate. He won't be able to measure it. He does not know how "diabetes/insulin" is said in Russian. These two keywords could save his life if he manages to make himself understood.

But what is the point of insurgency and the requirement of little more humane conditions of detention, since he is considered a less than nothing ?

The treatment he is undergoing seems to attest to this.

11 p.m.

One last pee for the night.

Jacob takes the opportunity to utter these two words essential to the preservation of his life :

" *Diabetic / Insulin* "

hoping that this will resonate to the ears of his guardians, hoping that these two words are spoken in the same way in Russian as in English.

Yes, he's right. "Diabetic" in English, is pronounced "Diabeticheskiy" in Russian.

Indeed, the two officers seem to have understood the message, this form of SOS that they cannot ignore and fail to report to the duty officer.

An hour later, under guard, a civilian doctor enters the room accompanied by the duty officer.

The civilian doctor seems shocked to see the conditions of detention of this American, (of whom he knows nothing), afraid by the prospect that this man could spend the night on a chair.

Before providing him care , he asks that Jacob be detached. He examines him summarily, measures his blood sugar rate, and then give him the necessary insulin dose needed to balance his blood sugar. There was a real urgency.

He also called for coverage and a less restrictive solution to allow the accused to stretch out his body for a few hours, considering his state of health.

The officer on duty makes the decision after a period of hesitation to arrange for a blanket to be provided in order than, Jacob could lie down for a few hours and rests.

On leaving, the civilian doctor gave to him (with the courtesy of   the duty officer), a few pieces of sugar for the next day just in case.

The idea of uttering the words "US Embassy" to the civilian doctor crossed his mind for a moment. But he does not know what the reprisals would be after the departure of the civilian doctor, especially since he still does not know what is reproached to him. He could make his case worse.

Reassured after receiving the care he needed, he sank into a deep sleep, almost forgetting his conditions of detention, lying on the floor, on a blanket.

20

Providence is at work.

Jacob's secret prayers nevertheless reached the ears of the one who welcomed the prodigal son with infinite goodness in his home upon his return.

Suddenly, in this very dark sky above his head, a glimmer seems to be drawing. He doesn't know it yet.

Indeed, on his way home in the middle of that dark night, the civilian doctor did not stop thinking about this American to whom he had just saved life.

He understands that he is deprived of his most basic rights, but when it comes to homeland security and a U.S. accused, his power is limited, even as a doctor.

So, after careful consideration, he stopped his car by a telephone booth and called a friend, a freelance journalist.

- " *Hello, Irina?* "

- " *Hello Andreï, what's going on? Why are you calling me so late?* "

- " *Can I talk to you for a minute?* "

- " *Yes Andreï. I'm worried about you!* "

- " *Do you know that the territorial security holds an American national at its premises in Novosibirsk?* "

- " *No Andreï I didn't know. First news. What did he do? ... What's his name? ... How do you know about this case?* "

- " *I can't answer any of those questions you ask me. All I can tell you is that, I was called urgently to give him insulin. He was on the verge of a coma. I was shocked to see the conditions under which he is being held. Can you do something with his embassy to find out more please? There's a real urgency.* "

- " *Yes Andreï. I'll see what I can do. Take care of yourself, my friend.* "

- " *Irina, I didn't call you. I didn't tell you anything. Isn't it?* "

- " *Don't worry about it! Good night*. "

- " *Good night Irina.*

After this unexpected conversation with her friend Dr. Andreï, Irina concentrates for a short time and then, searches for the phone number of the U.S. Embassy in Moscow on

My last night in Siberia

the web.

Despite the late hour, Irina tries to reach the embassy with the hope of reaching an official as soon as possible.

As a freelance journalist, this is a case that could bring her some notoriety especially if she is alone on the spot.

Alleged spy cases are always very "noisy" (with international repercussions) and for her, to be on this kind of case, means to get a good step ahead of her colleagues, and in a sovereign way.

21

Several attempts later, Irina managed to reach the head of the diplomatic emergency cell, cell open 24/7.

She told him the whole story by emphasizing the urgency of the situation of this American national detained in the clutches of homeland security.

The U.S. official considered the matter serious enough to refer it to her hierarchy, who in turn found it useful to wake up the ambassador who ordered the referral to the Ministry of the Interior.

For her part, in this meantime, Irina wrote a paper which she managed to sell to the independent newspaper with which she usually collaborates. The morning edition spreads the case on the front page.

In the early hours of the morning, Novossibirsk is aware of what is happening in the premises of the territorial security. Comments are rife in the coffee shops.

The Minister of the Interior had a heated conversation with the senior territorial security officer of Novossibirsk, accusing him of failing to protect absolute secrecy on this matter which should be classified as defence secrecy. He ordered that Jacob BILLIGER be released and placed under house arrest while the investigation continues. Finally, he requires a full report on the case before the end of the morning for the prime Minister.

Effervescence and big panic at the premises

of the territorial security. The senior officer wears his face of bad days. He summons his staff and demands explanations by screaming with all his might. The walls of his office can attest to this.

The only person outside the service who approached the accused was the civilian doctor who came to administer him insulin he needed.

The order was immediately given to check the calls made from the doctor's phone and his entourage, (his family included) in the last 24 hours.

No calls towards the U.S. Embassy in Moscow.

They cannot imagine who has called the embassy. An internal investigation is ordered. We have to find a culprit at all costs. Everyone receives an order with obligation of results, from the two guards who reported the onset of his diabetes crisis, and its possible complications (so that the responsabilities do not fall on them) to the officer on duty who brought a civilian doctor into the premises of the territorial security , who justifies himself by mentioning the urgency of the situation. The use of a military doctor would have required delays incompatible with the accused's state of health.

Disciplinary sanctions will fall down, warns the senior officer.

He does not want to take responsibility for this breach of rules.

In desperation, and in accordance with the orders of the Minister of the Interior against which no one can object, Jacob BILLIGER is released and taken back to his home where he is under house arrest until the end of the investigation.

This house arrest is accompanied by exit conditions only for basic necessities. The accused is also exceptionally allowed to take a daily walk of half an hour in the morning and afternoon in a perimeter not exceeding 1 km around his home. It is possible for him to receive a doctor's visit after informing the territorial security.

The passport is seized.

It's forbidden to go back to university.

22

After a long long shower during which every square centimeter of his skin was carefully cleaned up, Jacob went to bed and immediately plunged into a deep sleep for several hours.

He emerges from this long sleep late in the afternoon and wonders where he is. He looks around. He has trouble locating himself in space. Panic is not far away. Where are the two guards? He wonders. They're not here. He is not handcuffed.

Gradually he realizes that he is at home, in bed. He feels pain in his wrists. He extends his arms in front of him and looks at his wrists. He remembers everything. The handcuffs bruised his flesh and left in his mind an indelible memory. He's got a knotted throat. He has tears in his eyes but too proud to cry. That would give them too much honor.

He's thirsty.

He manages to stand up. His head is spinning a little. He's shaking. He walks cautiously towards the refrigerator. He has not quite regained his balance that faltered during his incarceration.

Suddenly stopped in his progress, he found himself in the position of the cyclist who is prevented from pedaling on his bike. As a result, he loses his balance and ends up on the ground. His priority is to get up, get back in the saddle and keep moving.

Twenty-four hours of an inhuman treatment is

enough to transform the character of a man, as strong, as determined as he can be.

He was in love with life. Now he could praise nothingness.

He was flabbergasted by the genius of men. Now he wonders about man's ability to discern what is from what is not.

He was the scholar. Now he feels ignorant of the simple rules of survival of his species.

He suddenly feels out of step. What he has just experienced is not in harmony with what he believes to know about the reality of man's relationship with his fellow human beings in society. He now knows that the bites of slander always leave scars, like a gash on the face that cannot hide or fade over time.

 He's in front of the refrigerator. He opens it. He takes out the bottle of spring water. He serves himself a big glass. A real treasure in his hands. Fresh water, flowing slowly down his throat.

With his glass in his hand, he sketches a few steps in this tiny apartment. He needs to regain possession of this place that suddenly seems so big to him since his stay in the cramped room of the territorial security.

He can come and go as he pleases, without having to ask permission.

Moments later, he settles back into the bed. His thought is again invaded by this case. Moreover, on reflection, he still does not know what he has done wrong to suffer this physical and pychological torture.

23

6.30 pm.

The phone on the landline starts ringing.
A little hesitant, he moves cautiously towards
the handset placed on the coffee table.

He picks up the handset.

- " *Hello!* "

- " *Hello Mr BILLIGER?* "

asks the caller in English.

- " *Yes, it's me Jacob BILLIGER who is speaking. Who are you?* "

- " *JOHNSON William, from the U.S. embassy in Russia. I'm calling from Moscow. Can we speak ?* "

- " *Delighted ! Happy to hear a friendly voice. ... Yes, I have all my time as you already know.* "

- " *Well, we just received a briefing note on your next hearing at the territory security premises in Novossibirsk, early tomorrow afternoon. We have found you a bilingual lawyer who will assist you during this hearing. We will be in close contact with him to follow up on this case.* "

- " *Do you have any questions?* "

- " *Yes I have a question.* "

- " *I'm listening to you, Mr. BILLIGER.* "

My last night in Siberia
© *Nathanaël AMAH , 2020 NATHAM Collection*

- " *Would I be handcuffed between two armed agents?* "

- " *No Mr. BILLIGER. Dont' worry. It's your lawyer who's going to pick you up from your home. Is that okay with you?* "

- " *It's ok Mr. JOHNSON. Thank you.* "

- " *Any more question?* "

- " *No, Mr. JOHNSON.* "

- " *Ok! Good evening Mr. BILLIGER. See you tomorrow.* "

- " *Good evening, Mr. JOHNSON.* "

Jacob hangs up.

He can't help but drink a glass of vodka. Then a second one.

Sudden surge in blood pressure. He has to go to bed. He's waiting to feel better. In the meantime, his communicator reflexes are taking over. On the eve of a conference, he has to review the content, imagine all the possible questions, try to find the right answers to establish or maintain his credibility in front of his audience. Choose the right suit, the right color. The clothes sometimes make the man contrary to the old saying, because what hides behind the soul of the one who wears these clothes, is above appearances.

24

In the early morning, Jacob received a call from the lawyer hired by the U.S. Embassy, who offered him to meet before the hearing and discuss the case over lunch.

He agreed.

The lawyer arrived at about 10:30 am in the apartment.

Master ALEKSANDR listened to Jacob's story, took some notes, asked him specific questions about the reasons for his presence in Novossibirsk, about his activities at the university, etc etc...

Jabob provided the most precise answers, with all the intelligence that characterizes him.

The lawyer was interested by this man named Igor, who according to his sources, never existed and who would be a pure invention of Jacob.

- " *Master, what exactly am I being blamed for in this case? Why this relentlessness against me?* "

- " *I do not know exactly, but everything seems to lead us towards a charge of spying, which is considered something very serious here.* "

- " *Spying??? Me ?* "

The lawyer sketches a smile.

- " Yes, everything seems to make you look like the perfect spy. "

- " You mean, the one who's in charge of secretly collecting secret documents and delivering information about a foreign power? "

- " Yes, exactly Sir ! "

- " Let me ask you a question, Master. "

- " Please. "

- " Did you listen to me well when I described at length the purpose of my mission at university? Did you understand the circumstances of my arrival in Siberia three months ago ? "

- " Yes, I listened carefully. But it seems that homeland security has a different version of your story. "

- " Another version ? "

- " Yes, Sir. It seems. "

- " **Which one ?** "

- " **I don't know. This is what you have to think logically, given the treatment that has been inflicted on you. Otherwise, why do you think they persecuted you as they did ?** "

25

Discussion continues at the restaurant.

- " ***What should I expect at the end of this hearing ?*** "

- " ***This hearing is held midway through the official investigation. It will be used to verify specific points identified during the official investigation. No confrontation or counter-investigation. They just want to validate some points before the final report.*** "

- " *As I understand it, I am already doomed?* "

- " *You know Mr. BILLIGER, if the preliminary inquiry does not reveal anything, you will no longer be worried.* "

- " *At worst, what would it be for me? What would be my fate ?* "

- " *Two options: 1/ depending on the severity, you will be thrown in jail for a long time and you will be the subject of a deal between my country and your country. 2/ If nothing is conclusive, so as not to lose face, you will be expelled from the country. In any case, you will be the subject of a wide publicity that will be relayed all over the world. You can say goodbye to your career.* "

- " *Would I have to answer the questions since everything will already be decided in advance ?* "

- " *Yes you must, otherwise it would be considered a contempt towards the members of commission. And in that case, you'll be*

My last night in Siberia

incarcerated. This will put an end to your reduced house arrest. The investigation will be at charge only. Do you see what I'm thinking of ? "

Jacob seems to have understood.

- " *As I understand it, must I consider this masquerade as the prelude of the end of my mission in the framework of the professors exchange program between Russia and the United States? "*

- " *I'm afraid mr BILLIGER. I don't want to give you false hope. State security is paramount in every country in the world. "*

Jacob stays silent.

- " *Well, Mr. BILLIGER, we have to eat now. In an hour we have to hit the road. Enjoy your meal. "*

- " *Enjoy your meal. "*

Lunch is quickly consumed, in a monastic silence.

Maybe the last one before a long time.

So he savored every bite. Every sip of this delicious vodka chosen by the lawyer, was an enchantment for the palate.

This supposed "last meal of the condemned" before confinement or expulsion (according to the options mentioned by the lawyer), is of particular importance.

Seen from the outside, such an appetite in such a perspective, can be surprising.

Emotion makes you hungry, they say.

What if appetite was necessary to smother grief at this particular moment in an individual's life, a prelude to a inevitable end?

26

2 pm.

Jacob and his lawyer enter the premises of the territorial security. They are on the list of visitors of the day. An armed officer, leads them in front of the audition room. He knocks on the door. Seconds later, the door is opened from the inside by an agent who asks them to enter.

The lawyer enters first, follow-up by the defendant Jacob BILLIGER. The officer closes the door behind them and returns to sit.

The lawyer :

- " *Ladies and gentlemen, good morning. I am master ALEKSANDR, Mr Jacob BILLIGER's lawyer. Here we are, in accordance with the terms of the summons that the Committee on Preliminary Hearings sent to us. We are willing to answer your questions..* "

In this courtroom, a dozen people (including three women), all sitting behind a large table, a thick folder placed in front of each of them, all dressed with civilian clothes, their faces closed, their eyes gazed on the defendant Jacob BILLIGER.

Opposite, two ordinary chairs, spread at least one metre apart, preventing the lawyer and the defendant from communicating between each other.

In fact, the lawyer is only there to attend the hearing. He has no real-time intervention during the hearing. His presence is an exceptional privilege granted to the Us State in the context of this hearing, to ensure that the rights of the accused BILLIGER have been strictly respected according to international conventions.

Jacob has been briefed for this purpose by his lawyer, and does not seem surprised or lost in the face of this legal provision implemented by the hearings committee.

He knows that his defence is up to him and that his future after this hearing will depend only on his ability to provide clarification, the appropriate responses to the charges against him.

His long experience as a speaker predisposes him to confront an audience not acquired to his cause, even hostile. But in this case, regardless of the quality of his performance before this commission, the final decision will not be his decision. Moreover, the major disadvantage of not knowing the grievances retained against him, *de facto* condemns him to surpass himself in his defence strategy before this committee.

He will have to find arguments that strike the spirits with their brutal sharpness, and which will produce a psychological shock that will shake the certainties of the members of this commission, for his rehabilitation which in his mind is not in doubt.

27

All the members of this commission are surprised, even destabilized, to see the defendant Jacob BILLIGER in an unexpected way.

For the majority of them, they have participated down in the past at dozens of auditions. In their soul and conscience, they never felt this feeling of not being in front of the person described in the thick file before each of them.

Some would say that the fate of the defendant Jacob BILLIGER presents itself under the best omens in the face of this commission.

But can homeland security afford the luxury of relying on the face, costume and innocent attitudes of a defendant suspected of threatening the security of the state?

The large majority of the active members, part of such a commission, are handpicked among former military personnel, who are graded by their service status, trained in the art of searching the depths of the most devious souls of individuals who are the subject of proven suspicions or not, to act against the security of the State.

Indeed, they discover a serene person, with an impassive face, flexible gestures, a perfectly balanced attitude, ready to face them to defend his honour, and who, to the general surprise, reviews for a few seconds, each of the faces, as to establish a connection with each of the people of this commission.

In doing so, he noticed that one of these people had looked down as he stared at her, unable to support his gaze.

This constitutes for him the "entry point" in this compact and impenetrable block that this commission forms in front of him.

Application of an old technique used by speakers in front of a difficult, even hostile audience.

Even if around this table, they are ten in front of him , he will only address that person throughout his hearing.

This person will be his only interlocutor regardless of the origin of the question put to him.

He will explain to her, he will take her as a witness, he will ask her to examine the facts from a more appropriate angle, he will ask her to put herself in his place, he will smile at her, he will make her admit that this hearing will give birth to a mouse and not a mountain, etc...

He will put his future in her hands, he will ask her not to condemn him if she has a reasonable doubt.

And in the end, he will express to her, his sincere thanks for having listen to him.

He won't take his eyes off her.

28

In a firm and strong voice, the chairperson of the committee declare :

- " *Vstrecha otkryta.* "
(the meeting is open)

And in impeccable English :

- " *Mr. Jacob BILLIGER, please stand up. I will proceed with the reading of the indictment.* "

Jacob stands up and listens religiously to the indictment.

He's knocked out but he's still impassive. He doesn't waver. He is firmly anchored to the ground.

He is a thousand kilometers away from imagining what he just has heard.

He variously is accused of his false agronomy skills, his presence on Russian soil for reasons other than those mentioned in the exchanges of professors between the United States and Russia, his membership in a subversive movement whose objective is to try to disrupt the established order, and to top it off, his repeated contacts with a so-called Igor who is actually called Anton, an activist longin the viewfinder of the territorial security, who has disappeared from radar in Moscow and appeared in Novosibirsk as by chance some time after his arrival from the United States.

Like a hyper-powerful computer, he structures his thinking and stands ready to defend himself.

So the questions are coming from all sides. A plethora of allegations against him. Recurring questions, ten times, twenty times asked in all forms.

Among the main ones :

- " *Why did you come to Novosibirsk ?* "

- " *Mr. BILLIGER, who do you work for?* "

- " *Did you give to Anton any documents? What documents did you give to Anton and why?* "

Like a warrior on a battlefield, his eye riveted on his single entry point, Jacob fights a fierce battle, alternately replying point to point, refuting, retaliating, retorting, and sometimes even, arguing.

It is a bloody battle at the end of which he still stands, his eyes sharp, his nostrils open, taking great breaths of oxygen to feed his heart put to the test, like a thoroughbred horse which has just run a steeplechase.

His lawyer included, all are unanimous in the face of this thunderbolt of war who defends his honor and reputation tooth and nail.

29

After three hours of this fierce battle, visibly short of arguments, the President whistles the end of the confrontation.

She ordered that a half bottle of water be given to him.

In Russian, the President announced to the lawyer that the conclusions of the hearing are under advisement for two weeks.

Jacob BILLIGER is free to return home, but he

is still prohibited from entering the university.

She declares the session over.

The lawyer thanks the commission and withdraws with his client.

Outside, master ALEKSANDR invites Jacob to have a drink in a vodka bar in the city centre.

Once settled, the two men debrief the hearing.

The lawyer admits that he was impressed by the relevance of Jacob's answers. For him, the acquittal will be prononced. Everything should be back to normal soon, but he urges caution during the two weeks during which the commission's decision is put on hold.

He reminds him, for all intents and purposes, that, as a general rule, the commission does not have a reputation for getting the wrong target. And if this is the case, the way out not to lose face, is the outright pronouncement of an order of expulsion from the territory, usually followed by the application of reciprocity decided by the country of the deportee if his status falls under the public service.

So this is an opportunity for the international media to wake up by interposed press, the old quarrels between Russia and its old enemy of always which are the United States of America.

- " ***Can a deportation order be appealed in this country?*** "

- " ***Everything related to the security of the state is subject to a unilateral decision.*** "

- " ***I got it. Thank you master, can you please drop me off at my home? I'm extremely tired. I need to rest.*** "

- " ***Don't worry, Mr. BILLIGER.*** "

30

Arriving at the apartment, very calmly, Jacob undressed, took a shower and went to bed.

The next morning when you wake up, a few stretching movements. His body is knotted, his muscles sore, worse than if he had run two marathons on a one-on-one run.

He does not think about anything. He tries to empty his head.

This whole day must be devoted to decompensate. Nothing should pollute his mind.

He prepares his breakfast. He settles down and takes advantage of this peace to enjoy his cup of coffee and his salted butter toasts. A few red berries to strengthen his immune system and another cup of coffee.

Although he was deprived of his laptop, he took his notepad and began to define the main features of the document for which the project director had requested his help.

It's not very complicated for him to do this job. He is very good at the subject and, as he should soon return to university, so he might as well take a little ahead.

His performance the day before reinforces his idea that soon everything will be back to normal and that he will come out of this nightmare with his head held high. He is deeply convinced of this.

The morning passed very quickly.

A quick shower then, a few shopping at the grocery store.

He cannot exceed a one-kilometre radius around his home. Therefore, he takes advantage of every metre traveled. He looks everywhere. He discovers the street smells . He analyzes them. He discovers his neighborhood.

On the way back, he washes a few socks, two or three underwear while waiting for lunch to finish cooking.

Two weeks is a long time. He needs to keep himself busy   physically and mentally.

31

A week and a half after his hearing, at around 7 p.m., Jacob was visited by two homeland security officers, who were in charge to deliver to him by hand, an deportation order from the territory. Sentence that should be executed the next day at 6 a.m. The territorial security will return to escort him to the airport. His passport and laptop will be returned to him at the airport.

After making him sign a receipt, they went

away.

He closed the door behind them.

Jacob read the contents of this document written in English, without frowning, then put the leaflet back in its envelope and put it all on the coffee table of the living room.

Very calmly, he kept busy preparing his dinner, then settled down with his meal tray in front of the television.

While having dinner, he follows the programs on CNN.

The next day, at 6 a.m., three territorial security officers, including one armed with a Kalashnikov, a representative of the U.S. Embassy, show up at the door of Jacob's apartment.

They ring once, twice, three times. There's no answer. They wait a short time, then do it again. There's no answer.

The man who seems to lead the group, orders

My last night in Siberia

his colleague to go to pick up the janitor.

This one arrives a little breathless, the curlers still in the hair, equipped with a set of keys.

A new series of attempts later, the concierge received the order to open the door.

She obeys.

With her hand trembling, she managed to unlock the door. The security has not been positioned.

The armed officer pushs her away with the tip of his weapon, and enters the apartment first and immediately gets out, frightened.

- " *Ublyudok ubil sebya !* "
(The son of a bitch committed suicide !)

  he said.

The others don't believe. They rush into the apartment and discover the horrific scene.

In the illuminated livingroom, in front of the

TV still on, Jacob BILLIGER sits with his head bent back, lifeless.

On the meal tray, next to his plate and cutlery, an empty bottle of vodka, a flask of sleeping pills brought back from Chicago, emptied of its contents.

By leaning towards him to check his pulse, the commando leader discovers a paper placed next to him in the sofa, on which it's written in English :

" *Someone wrote a long time ago : It is better to keep the nostalgia of a paradise by leaving it rather than to turn it into hell by staying there.*

I passionately loved my job. I exercised it with respect and honesty.

I am innocent of what I am accused of.

I shouted it out loud.

No one listened to me.

So I leave, without regret or sorrow.

My honor is safe, my reputation intact.
Tonight is my last night in SIBERIA.
Mom, I love you. Forgive me.

JACOB BILLIGER, Professor Emeritus. "

Epilogue

Thus ended on the land of Russia, the life of this extraordinary professor.

Jacob BILLIGER, born to live this exciting life as a researcher, went away with his quiet conscience and his undiminished reputation.

He leaves behind a colossal work and the memory of a man with a sharp mind, whose face continually shows a devastating smile.

How many Jacob BILLIGER around the world, who did not wake up one morning, preferring to leave life, so as not to have to defend themselves against the devastations of slander ?

END.

My last night in Siberia

My last night in Siberia

My last night in Siberia

Éditor : BoD-Books on Demand, 12/14 rond point des
Champs Élysées, 75008 Paris, France
Impression: BoD-Books on Demand, Norderstedt,
Allemagne
ISBN : 9782322240364
Dépôt légal : August, 2020

My last night in Siberia